SO-EIH-691

Owl's Eyes &
Seeking a Spirit

Kootenai Indian Stories

Owl's Eyes & Seeking a Spirit

Kootenai Indian Stories

Developed by the
Kootenai Culture Committee
Confederated Salish and Kootenai Tribes

1981 Committee Staff:
Cleo Kenmille, Coordinator
Glen James
Madeline Couture
Sarah Bufton
Sophie Matt
Sarah Eneas
Patricia Hewankorn
Joseph Antiste, Consultant
Oshanee Kenmille, Consultant
Debbie Joseph Finley, Illustrator
Howard Kallowat, Jr., Illustrator

Co-published by
Salish Kootenai College Press, Pablo, Montana
&
Montana Historical Society Press, Helena, Montana

Originally published as KOOTENAI STORIES in THE INDIAN READ-
ING SERIES by the Pacific Northwest Indian Program, Joseph Coburn,
Director, Northwest Regional Educational Laboratory, Portland, Oregon.

Cover drawing by Debbie Joseph Finley.
Cover design by Wyatt Designs, Helena, MT.

Library of Congress Cataloging-in-Publication Data:

Owl's eyes.
    Owl's eyes & Seeking a spirit : Kootenai Indian stories / developed by the
Kootenai Culture Committee, Confederated Salish and Kootenai Tribes ; Debbie Jo-
seph Finley, illustrator ; Howard Kallowat, Jr., illustrator.
    p. cm.
    Summary: Two traditional tales recorded by Kootenai elders and illustrated by
Kootenai artists from the Flathead Indian Reservation in western Montana.
    ISBN 0-91729-866-7 9 pbk. : alk. paper)
    1. Kutenai Indians–Folklore. 2. Tales–Montana. 3. Legends–Montana. [1. Kutenai
Indians–Folklore. 2. Indians of North America–Montana–Folklore. 3. Folklore–Mon-
tana.] I. Title. II. Title: Owl's eyes and Seeking a spirit. III. Title: Owl's eyes. IV.
Title: Kootenai Indian stories. V. Finley, Debbie Joseph, ill. VI. Kallowat, Howard,
ill. VII. Confederated Salish and Kootenai Tribes of the Flathead Reservation. Kootenai
Culture Committee. VIII. Title: Seeking a spirit.

E99.K85 O9 1999
398.2'089'973 21–dc21   99-041884

All rights reserved. No part of this publication may be reproduced or trans-
mitted in any form or by any means, electronic or mechanical, including
photocopy, recording, or any information storage or retrieval system, with-
out permission in writing from the copyright holder.

Copyright 1981 Kootenai Culture Committee, Elmo,
Montana

This printing reset and reprinted 2000 by
Salish Kootenai College Press
Box 117
Pablo, MT 59855
&
Montana Historical Society Press
Box 201201
Helena, MT 59620

Owl's Eyes & Seeking a Spirit

Kootenai Indian Stories

Owl's Eyes

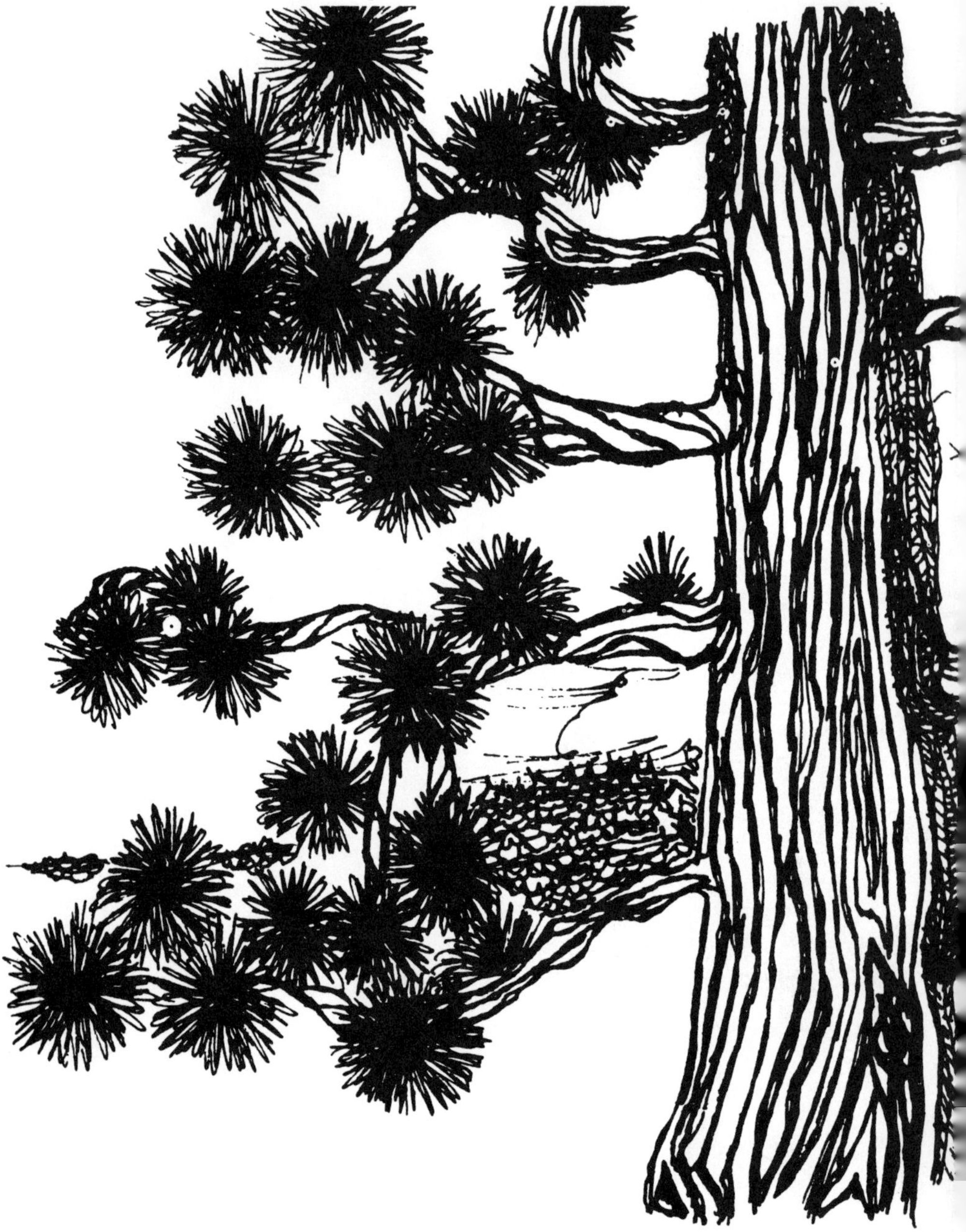

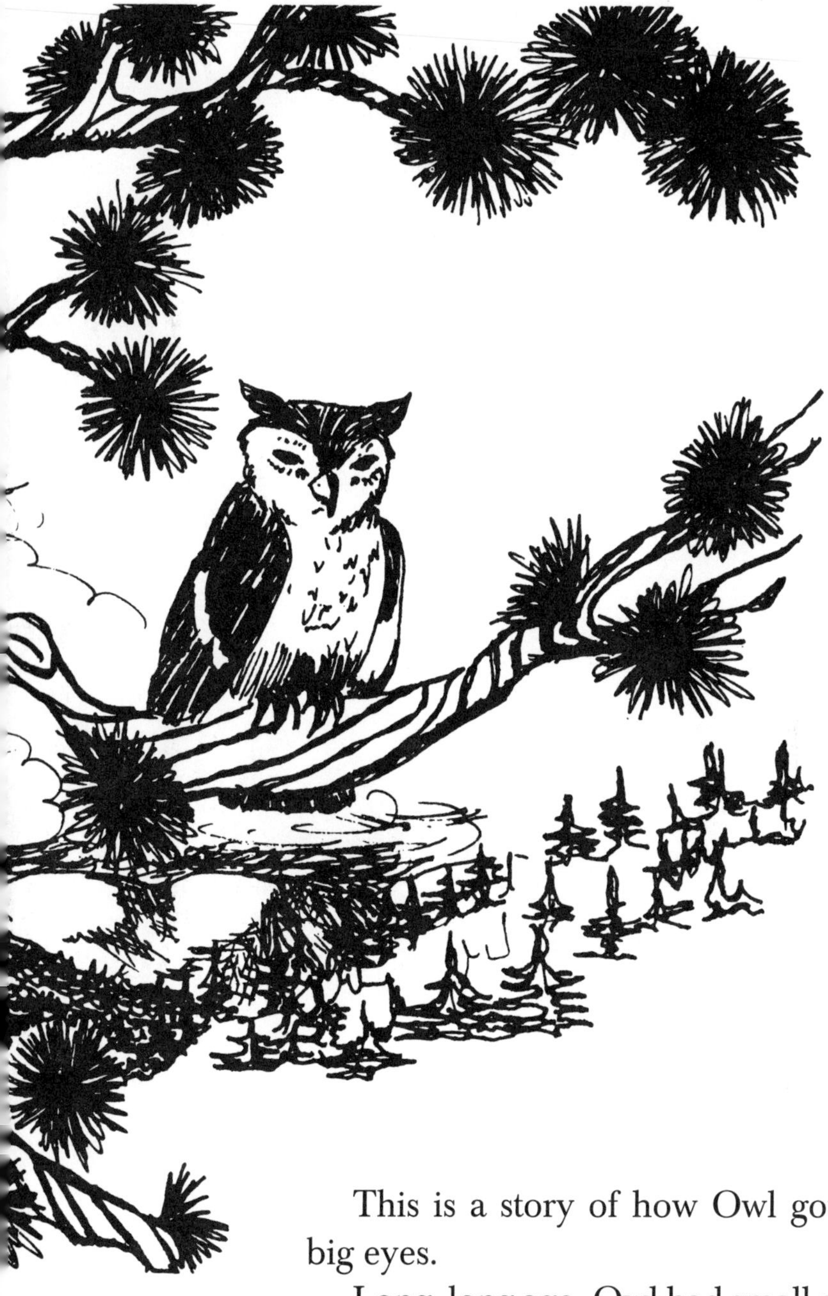

This is a story of how Owl got his big eyes.

Long, long ago, Owl had small eyes. Owl would spend most of his time sitting high in the trees.

Owl had a friend whose name was
Mouse. Owl and Mouse always played
together.

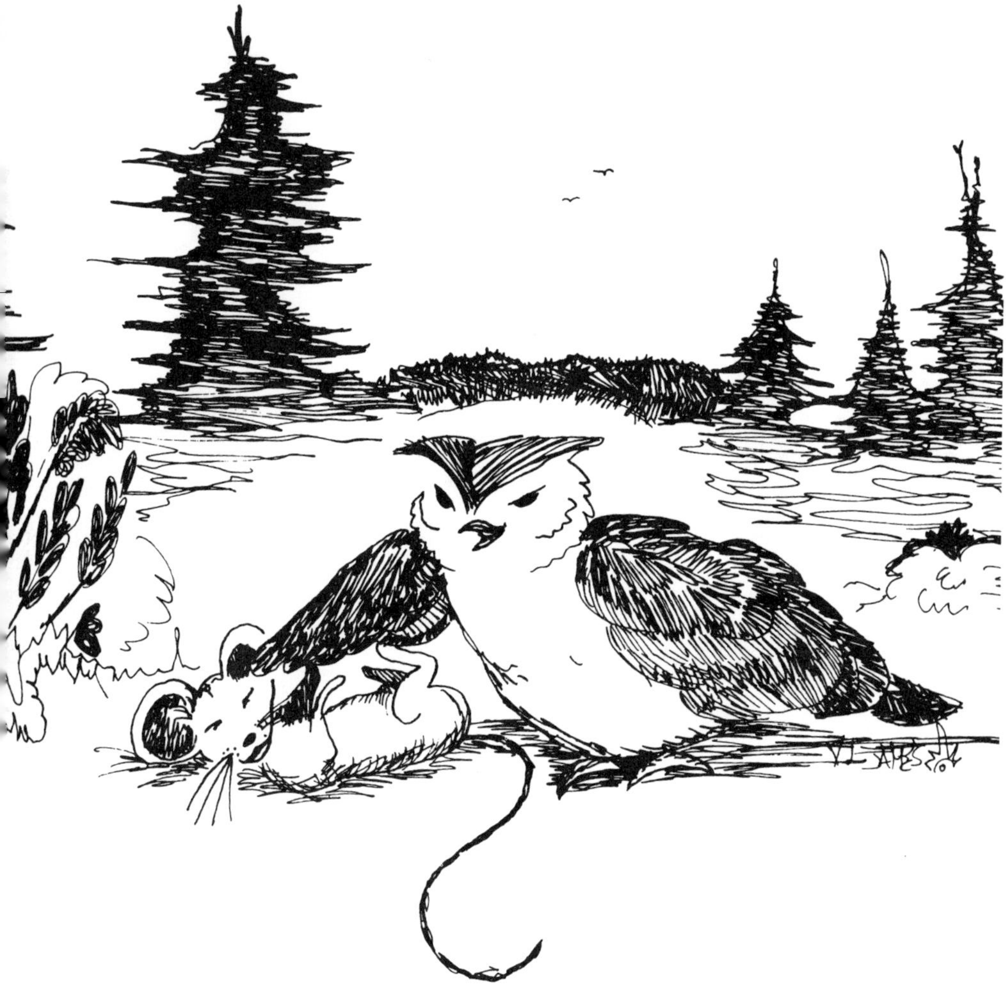

One night Owl was sitting high in his tree. Mouse called to Owl, "Owl, please come down and play with me." Owl never heard his tiny friend because he was sound asleep.

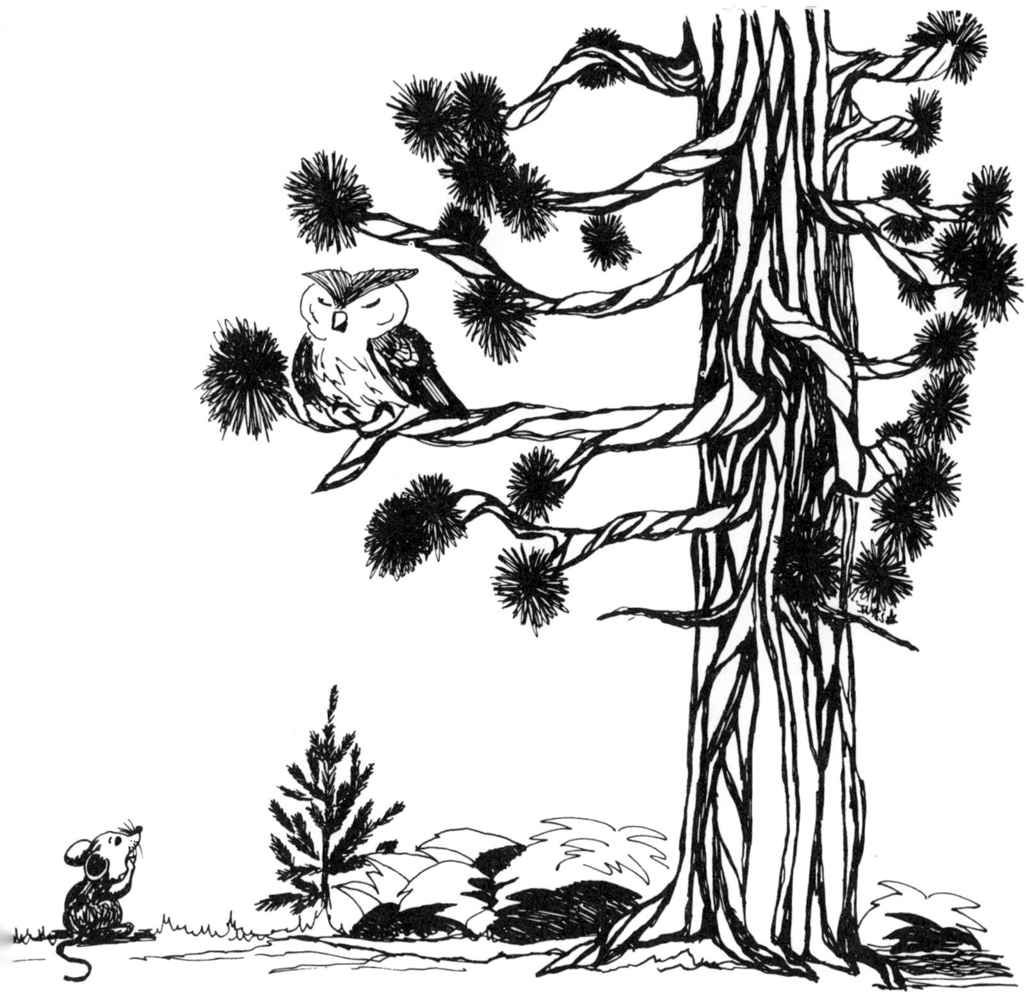

Nearby, Mr. Snake was quietly crawling through the grass. He heard Mouse crying. "Oh Owl, won't you come down and play with me?" Mouse cried.

Quietly, Mr. Snake slithered over to Mouse. When Mouse turned around and saw Mr. Snake, he screamed!

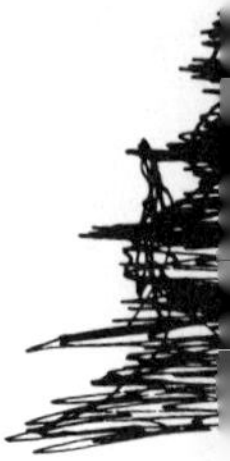

Mouse screamed so loud he woke up Owl. When Owl looked down for his little friend, it was too late. He saw Mr. Snake gobble Mouse up!

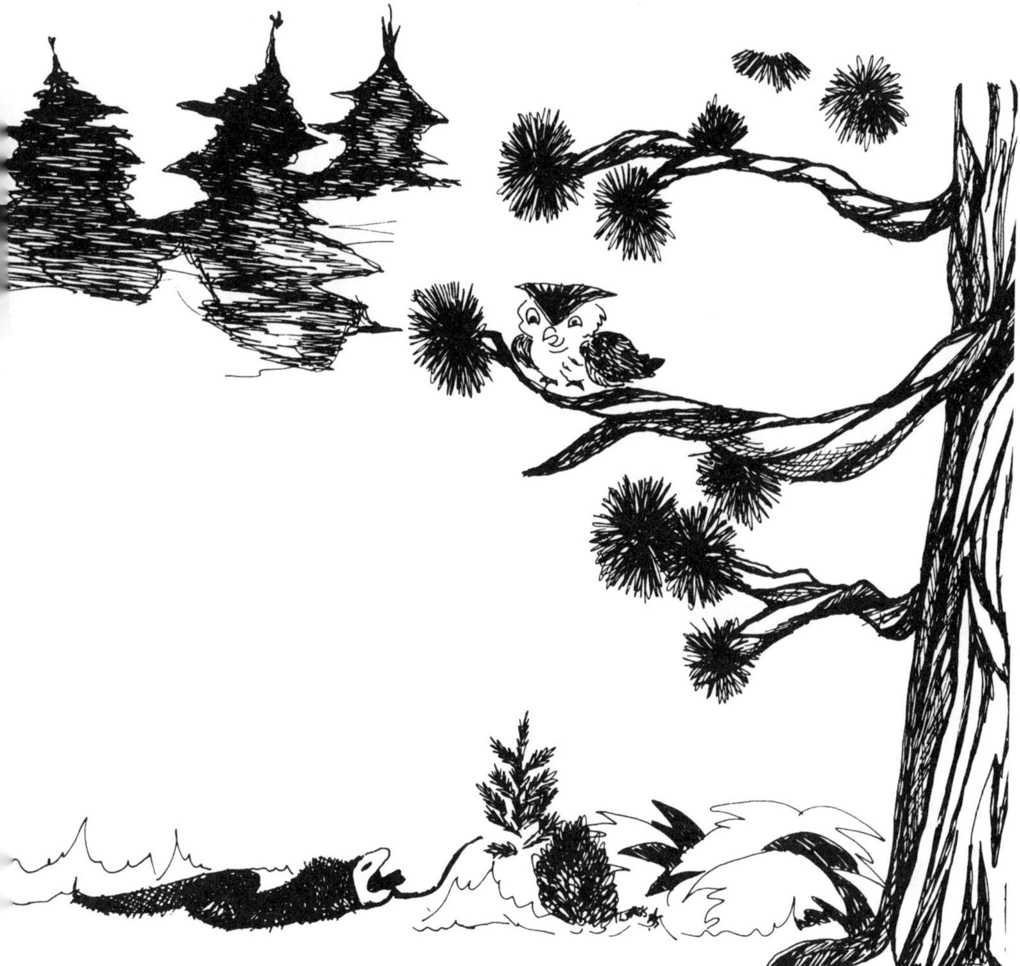

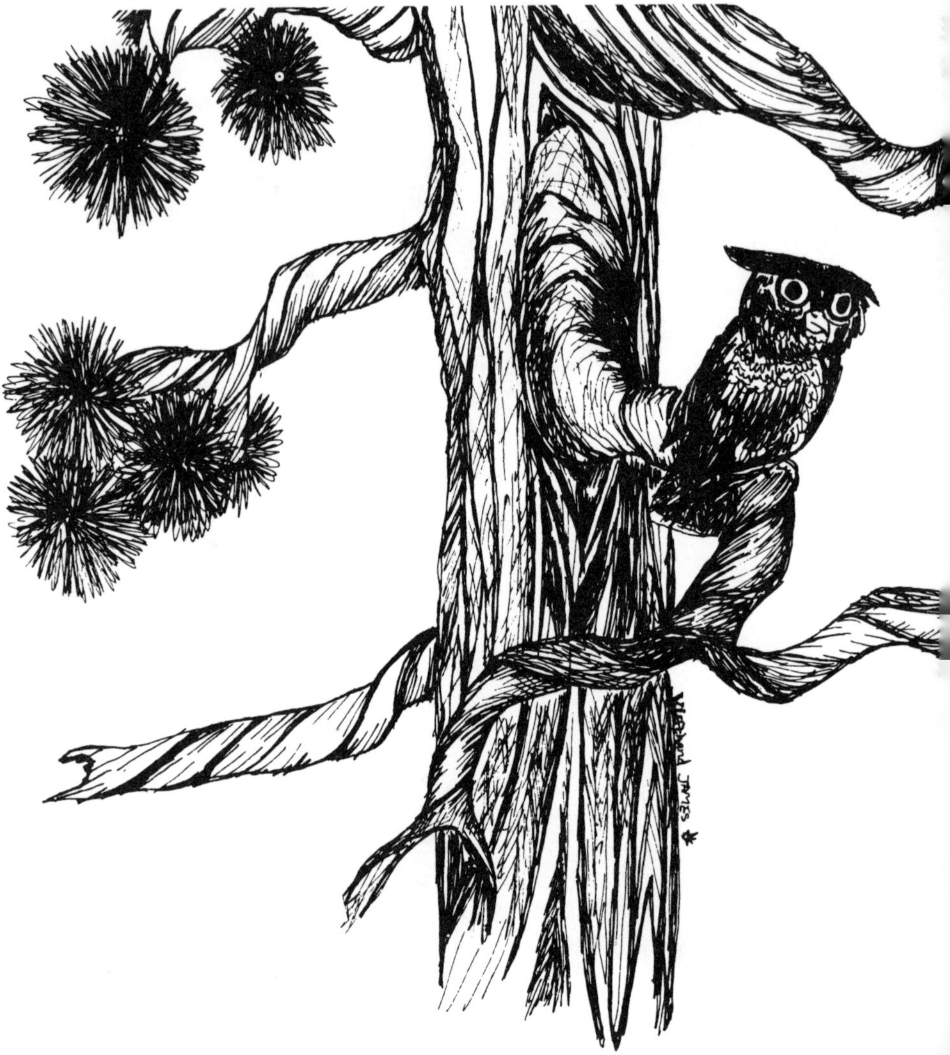

There wasn't a thing Owl could do. His tiny friend was gone.

Owl was so surprised he opened his eyes wider and wider. This is how Owl got his big eyes.

Seeking A Spirit

Long ago, there lived a young Kootenai boy whose name was Lassaw.

One day Lassaw left home and went to the top of a mountain. Lassaw wanted to seek a spirit. While Lassaw stayed on the mountain, he could not have any food or water.

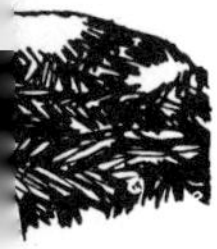

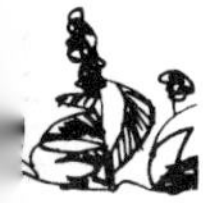

After two days and nights Lassaw cut off the tip of his finger. He tore his shirt and used it to make a bandage.

Lassaw prayed. He told the Great Spirit his finger hurt very much. Lassaw said, "Help me. Give me something so I can become a great medicine man."

Lassaw's finger was bleeding. His bandage was soaked. Because his finger hurt very much, he pressed his hand to his side.

Suddenly, Lassaw saw a buffalo! The buffalo was drinking water. Lassaw knew there was no water nearby. The buffalo continued to drink and when it was finished, it looked at Lassaw.

The buffalo spoke to Lassaw in the Kootenai language. It told Lassaw, "I know you are hurt. I came to help you. Whatever you ask for, I will give you."

The buffalo disappeared. Lassaw had
seen the spirit of the buffalo. He knew the
buffalo's spirit would always help him.

Lassaw became a great buffalo hunter.
He lived a long and a happy life.

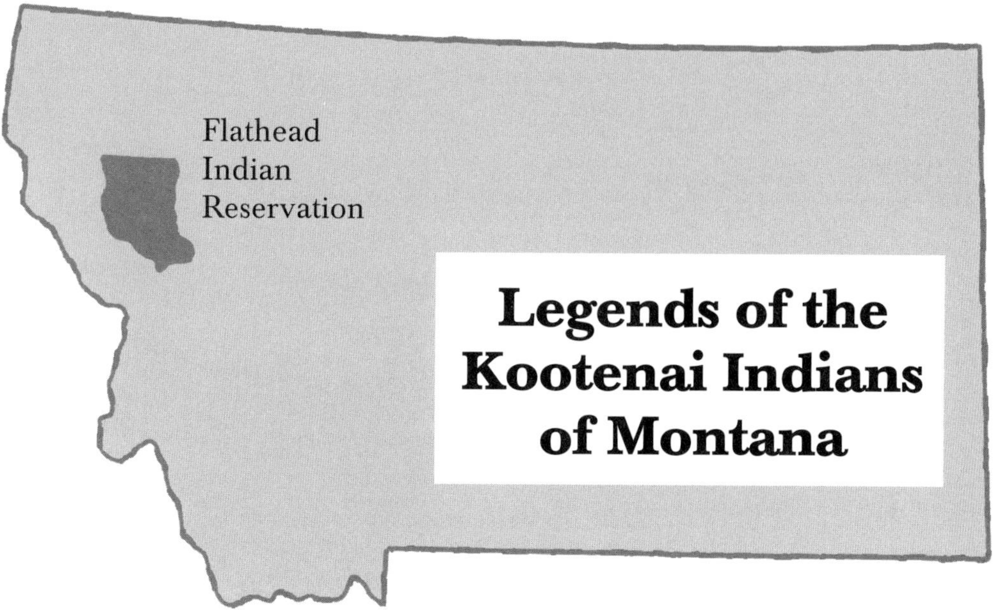
Flathead
Indian
Reservation

Legends of the Kootenai Indians of Montana

The Kootenai or Ksanka Nation is home in the Northern Rocky Mountains centered in what is now northern Montana, northern Idaho, and southeastern British Columbia. Our band is the southernmost of the seven Kootenai bands and resides on the Flathead Indian Reservation in northwest Montana.

Fish were abundant in the rivers and lakes; deer, buffalo, and other game were in the mountains and plains; and berries and roots filled these valleys. It is a vast area, but our people traveled easily with canoes, horses, and dogs. For centuries the Kootenai lived with the abundance of this land and cared for it.

Stories and games taught the young the values and wisdom of the elders. Some of these stories explained how greed, arrogance, and failure to respect the tribal community would lead to disgrace. Other legends taught about the habits and characteristics of the game animals that supported the tribe. The stories were entertainment, but they were also education. Storytelling was especially important during the winter when nights were long and cold in the Northern Rocky Mountains.

Through this book, these stories are now available to children everywhere, to share in the traditional values of Kootenai Indian storytellers.